A DINOSAUR NAMED

SUE ™

© The Field Museum 1997

THE FIND OF THE CENTURY

Acknowledgments

Amy Louis and Sharon Sullivan of the SUE Project at The Field Museum

Cheryl Carlesimo of Stone House Productions

Susan Hendrickson

The Photography Department of The Field Museum

The Black Hills Institute for permission to use their photos

The SUE Project was made possible in part by the generous support of the McDonald's® Corporation. 🄼

With special thanks to Brian Cooley for permission to use his sculpture of SUE on the cover of this book.

ISBN: 978-0-439-09983-7

Photography and illustration credits:

Cover: The Field Museum, Neg# GEO86199c, photograph by John Weinstein, sculpture by Brian Cooley; cover illustration inset by Portia Sloan, cover photograph inset from The Field Museum, Neg# GN89147.3c, photograph by John Weinstein; pages 3 and 48: The Field Museum, Neg# GEO86160-3c, photograph by John Weinstein; page 4: photograph provided courtesy of Black Hills Institute of Geological Research Inc., Hill City, South Dakota; page 5: illustration by Portia Sloan; page 7: photograph provided courtesy of Black Hills Institute of Geological Research Inc.; pages 8-9: photograph © Susan Hendrickson provided courtesy of Black Hills Institute of Geological Research Inc.; pages 10,11,13, 14: photographs provided courtesy of Black Hills Institute of Geological Research Inc.; page 15: illustration by Portia Sloan; page 16: Neg. No. 17808 courtesy Dept. of Library Services, American Museum of Natural History; page 17: Neg. No. 17811 courtesy Dept. of Library Services, American Museum of Natural History; pages 18-19: illustration by Portia Sloan; pages 20-21: illustration courtesy of the Science Team of the Field Museum; page 22: illustration by Portia Sloan; page 23: The Field Museum, Neg# GEO85737_9c, photograph by James Balodimas; pages 24-25: The Field Museum, Neg# CK9T, Charles R. Knight, artist; pages 27 and 29: illustration by Portia Sloan; page 31: photograph provided courtesy of Black Hills Institute of Geological Research Inc.; page 33: illustration by Portia Sloan; pages 34-37: photographs provided courtesy of Black Hills Institute of Geological Research Inc.; page 38: The Field Museum, Neg# GEO86127_2c, photograph by John Weinstein; page 39: The Field Museum, Neg# GN88582_3c, photograph by John Weinstein; page 40: The Field Museum, Neg# GN88863_36c, photograph by John Weinstein; page 41: The Field Museum, Neg# GN88584_10c, photograph by John Weinstein; page 42 (upper): The Field Museum, Neg# GN88688_35Ac, photograph by John Weinstein; page 42 (lower): The Field Museum, Neg# GN88766_23c, photograph by John Weinstein; page 43 (upper): The Field Museum, Neg# GN89035_3c, photograph by John Weinstein; page 43 (lower): The Field Museum, Neg# GN88688_25Ac, photograph by John Weinstein; page 44: The Field Museum, Neg# GN88582_66c, photograph by John Weinstein; page 45: The Field Museum, Neg# GEO86129_49c, photograph by John Weinstein; page 47: The Field Museum, Neg# GN88486_30Ac, photograph by Kimberly Mazanek.

Library of Congress Cataloging-in-Publication Data available

38 37 36 35 34 33   19 20

Printed in the U.S.A.   40
First printing, November 1999

SCHOLASTIC INC. AND THE FIELD MUSEUM PRESENT

A DINOSAUR NAMED

© The Field Museum 1997

THE FIND OF THE CENTURY

by Fay Robinson
with the SUE Science Team *of* The Field Museum

Christopher A. Brochu, John J. Flynn, Peter Laraba, Olivier C. Rieppel, and William F. Simpson

with illustrations by Portia Sloan

**This Scholastic Reader was produced
through the cooperation of the following:**

STONE HOUSE
PRODUCTIONS, LLC

SCHOLASTIC INC.

South Dakota

A Strange Day

There is a place in North America where rolling hills and tumbling cliffs cover the land. In the summer, temperatures soar to over 100 degrees. Dry, dusty winds blow.

In this place, western South Dakota, Susan Hendrickson camped out with her dog, Gypsy. It was the summer of 1990. Susan had been living out of a tent for six weeks. Every day, she worked outside in the blazing sun. Why would anyone choose to do that? Susan is a fossil hunter. South Dakota is one of the best places in the world to find fossils such as dinosaur bones.

Susan was with a group of fossil hunters from a company called the Black Hills Institute. The group had spent most of that summer digging up duck-billed dinosaurs called Edmontosaurus [ed-MON-toh-SORE-us]. Summer was almost over. Everyone was tired and ready to go home.

With just two days left, the group woke up to a thick fog. They could hardly see. The air was cool and still. "There is never fog in South Dakota in the summer time. It was such a strange day," Susan recalls.

This unusual day ended up being more amazing than anyone could have imagined.

CHAPTER 1

The Discovery

It all began with a flat tire. The tire on the group's truck had to be fixed. There is no getting around this rugged area of South Dakota without good tires on your truck.

Susan decided to stay behind while the others went to town to get a new tire. She was thinking about the cliffs across the valley. The group had carefully searched most of that area, but not all of it. "There was one little place I really wanted to go to, but there had been no time. We had been so busy," Susan remembers. This was her chance.

Susan and Gypsy set off to the rocky area. They hiked seven miles for more than two hours through the thick fog.

By the time they got there, the fog had burnt away. Susan did what fossil hunters always do when searching cliffs. She walked around the bottom first. She looked for bones that might have fallen downhill. She watched for the dull brown color of fossil bones among the gray rocks. After

fifteen minutes she hadn't found anything.

Then, Susan says, "All of a sudden, I saw a couple of two-inch pieces of bone and a bunch of little broken bone pieces." She looked up to see where the bone came from. Eight feet above, more bones jutted out of the cliff.

Susan climbed up for a closer look. She saw three huge backbones, a rib bone, and a leg bone. Because the broken edges of the bones were sticking straight out of the cliff, Susan could tell there were more bones inside. "I had never found more than small parts of T. rex before — some teeth and a couple of small pieces of bone. So I was really excited," Susan recalls.

Susan looked closely at the bones. They were hollow. Dinosaurs that ate meat, called carnivores, had hollow bones. Plant-eating dinosaurs, called herbivores, didn't. So this was a carnivore. And these bones were huge. "I knew the only large carnivorous dinosaur that lived in that area was the Tyrannosaurus rex," says Susan. "And I thought, 'Wow!'" At that time, only parts of eleven other Tyrannosaurus rex skeletons had ever been found.

Susan picked up two pieces of bone. She hurried back with Gypsy at her heels. She showed the others and told them what she had seen. They all agreed. There was a T. rex buried in those hills! They decided to name the dinosaur Sue, in honor of its discoverer.

Almost 30 feet of rock on top of the skeleton had to be cleared away before all of Sue's bones could be uncovered. But some of the people in the group had to go home. That left only three or four people to do this enormous job.

Using shovels, picks, and crow bars, the group got to work. From dawn to dusk, thirteen hours a day, they chipped and dug and broke away the cliff. They pushed 100 pound pieces of rock down the hill with their hands. The temperature rose above 120 degrees. The diggers were exhausted. But the excitement of what they hoped to find drove them on.

Soon the jumble of Sue's bones was exposed. The group quickly realized how unbelievable this Tyrannosaurus rex was. Almost all of the bones were there! Most dinosaur skeletons that are found are missing many, if not most, of their bones.

The creature's skull was the size of a refrigerator. Most of the teeth were set in its jaw, some twelve inches or longer from root to tooth tip. Its right front arm was there — one of only two T. rex arms ever discovered. Thirty-six tail

bones circled around the remains — one of the most complete T. rex tails ever found.

Often, fossil bones are chipped or broken apart. Sue's bones were nearly perfect. To top it off, Sue was huge. "It was really amazing," says Susan Hendrickson. "She just kept getting better and better. We were all in such shock. You can't ever dream of finding something so good and so big!" This was the find of a lifetime — the largest and most complete T. rex ever discovered.

Edge of cliff face where Susan Hendrickson found the first bones (see photos on pp. 10-11).

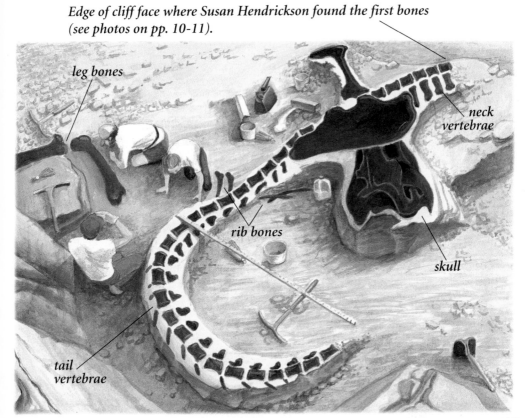

leg bones

neck vertebrae

rib bones

skull

tail vertebrae

CHAPTER 2

T. rex: What's the Story?

A man named Barnum Brown found the first Tyrannosaurus rex fossils in 1900. He brought the bones to his boss, Henry Osborn of the American Museum of Natural History. When Mr. Osborn saw the huge jaws and dagger-like teeth, he knew this was one powerful dinosaur. He named the species Tyrannosaurus rex, which means 'tyrant lizard king.' A tyrant is a mean, powerful leader. Over time, Tyranno-saurus rex has taken on the nickname T. rex.

T. rex stood about 40 feet long and 13 feet high at the hips. That's bigger than a city bus. Scientists think a T. rex may have weighed anywhere from two to seven tons.

Barnum Brown (left) and Henry Osborn (right)
at a dig site in Wyoming in 1897.

Its head alone might have weighed one ton. (One ton is 2,000 pounds — about what a small rhinoceros weighs.)

T. rex walked with its huge head forward. Its heavy tail, held off the ground, helped it keep its balance. The arms of T. rex were only as long as an adult human's arms. But they were very, very strong.

The jaws of a T. rex flashed as many as 58 teeth. It had the longest teeth of any known dinosaur. Up to five inches of tooth showed, from jaw to pointy tip. Including the roots, some teeth were longer than twelve inches! T. rex's teeth fell out and new ones grew back throughout its life.

Tyrannosaurus rex is a species of North American dinosaur. As of 1998, twenty-two specimens have been found—all in Canada or the western United States.

Sue has more of her bones preserved than any of the other T. rex skeletons. (The dinosaurs you see in museums have many "bones" made of plaster. Sometimes museums use parts of two or more T. rex skeletons to make one whole skeleton.)

Sue is 90 percent complete. Most of the other T. rex skeletons are less than half complete. Here is one way to understand. Imagine you have a ten-piece puzzle. But half the pieces are missing — five of them. Could you

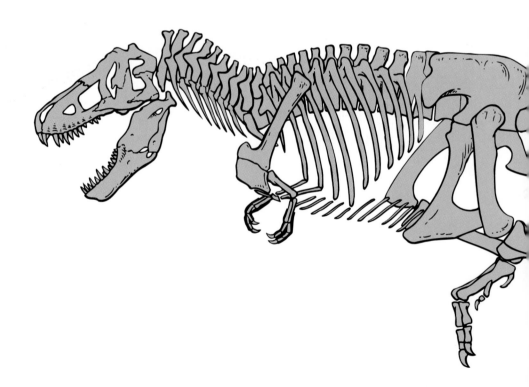

put the puzzle together? Could you tell what your finished puzzle would look like? Next, imagine you have nine out of ten pieces. You could probably put the puzzle together. And you'd have a good idea of what the finished puzzle would look like. Now think of the puzzle pieces as dinosaur bones!

With so many nearly perfect bones to study, scientists have the chance to learn more than ever about the species T. rex. And they have a chance to learn something about the life of one T. rex — Sue.

CHAPTER 3

The Life and Times of Sue

Sue lived about 67 million years ago. This was near the end of a time called the Cretaceous [kre-TAY-shus] period. The age of the dinosaurs was almost over. What was life like for Sue? If we could travel back in time, this is what we might see....

Reptiles were everywhere. In the air, pterosaurs [TER-o-sores] the size of small planes soared. In the water, long-necked plesiosaurs [PLEE-zee-o-sores] used their flippers to "fly" through the water. Sue roamed the land with other kinds of dinosaurs: the three-horned Triceratops [try-SER-rah-tops], the duck-billed hadrosaurs [HAD-ra-sores] such as the horn-crested Parasaurolophus [PAR-uh-sore-OL-uh-fus],

speedy, meat-eating Troodon [TRO-a-don], and armor-covered ankylosaurs [AN-key-lo-sores], built like tanks.

The ancestors of many animals alive today lived alongside Sue. Turtles and salamanders skittered in and out of the water. Jellyfish shared the seas with sharks and rays. Birds flew the skies. And on land, beetles and opossums crept about.

The weather was warmer then. In Sue's area, the air was humid and winters were mild. Sue probably never saw snow or ice. Sun-warmed rivers and shallow seas covered much of the

A 1920's classical interpretation of Tyrannosaurus rex and Triceratops by painter Charles Knight, from the collection of the Field Museum.

land. Sudden storms caused floods, sometimes burying dinosaurs under mud and sand.

The world around Sue was lush and green. Ferns, palms, and creeping vines covered the ground. Flowering plants bloomed all around. Smaller trees lived at the water's edge. Nearby, great forests grew. Giant relatives of today's fir trees reached toward the sky.

Based on what scientists know about the closest living relatives of T. rex—birds and reptiles—Sue probably hatched from an egg. Reptiles never stop growing. Since T. rex was a species of reptile, Sue grew her whole life long.

It is possible that Sue traveled alone. In search of food, she might have followed bellowing herds of hadrosaurs. Or maybe she waited behind trees, watching as thousands of Triceratops trudged by.

How did Sue catch and eat her meals? Most scientists think T. rex was a fierce hunter. If that is the case, we can imagine something like this....

A herd of Triceratops marches by. Sue watches from a distance. An older Triceratops, weak and sick, strays from the herd. Sue waits until the Triceratops is well behind the others. Then, Sue runs quickly from the bushes, catching the Triceratops by surprise. Although the Triceratops tries to run away, Sue is faster. She opens her mouth wide. Her jaws clamp down on the back of the Triceratops. Sue holds on tightly as the Triceratops thrashes. The Triceratops turns its head, its long horns pointing at Sue's ribs. Sue bites down again. This time she uses the hook-like claws on her arms to hold the Triceratops still. Soon the Triceratops is too weak to fight anymore. And Sue eats a very big dinner.

Not everyone agrees that T. rex was an active hunter. Some scientists think they ate animals that were already dead. These scientists think T. rex was too big to run fast. Their arms were too short to grab anything. And using their mouths as weapons would have been clumsy. If that is the case, we might imagine Sue ate this way....

A herd of Triceratops stops to feed at the water's edge. An old Triceratops, too weak to keep up, lies down and dies. A couple of days later, Sue wanders nearby. She sniffs the air and recognizes the smell of a dead animal. She follows the smell until she finds the old Triceratops. Using her strong jaws and teeth, she tears chunks of flesh and bone from the body. A Troodon dashes over to share Sue's meal. Sue faces the smaller dinosaur, opens her mouth wide, and roars. The Troodon runs away, frightened by Sue's size and teeth. Then Sue finishes her meal.

Scientists haven't decided which way T. rex ate. Maybe, like today's lions and sharks, they hunted live animals and ate the meat of dead animals. Some scientists think this is the best explanation.

No one knows how long a Tyrannosaurus rex lived. Some scientists think they lived about 30 years. Others have said they might have lived 60 years or more.

We don't know exactly how old Sue was when she died, although she did live many years. And we don't know yet what caused her death. But we do know what happened after she died.

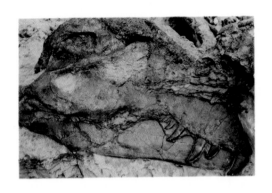

CHAPTER 4

Sue Becomes a Fossil

In order for bones to become fossils, they must be buried quickly. Otherwise hungry animals could carry them away. Or weather and time would cause them to rot. We know Sue's body was buried quickly because so many of her bones were found together. And because Sue's bones were found in sandstone, we know she got covered by sand.

Here's what might have happened to Sue. Maybe a sudden storm caused a flood. The flood waters carried mud and sand which buried Sue's body. Or maybe Sue died next to the river. Either way, her body was buried quickly. Her flesh soon rotted away, leaving her bones. Sand and mud from the flowing river covered them.

Sue's bones got a little jumbled up along the way. Her skull came off her spine. Her leg bones and ribs were scattered nearby. We know this because this was how her skeleton was found. (Usually, dinosaur fossils are much more jumbled and broken than Sue's. This is another sign that Sue's bones were buried very quickly.)

Sue's body was buried by layers of sand and mud. When sand and mud collect and settle, it is called sediment.

Thousands of years passed. The weight of all that was on top of Sue sealed her into the earth. The sand around her changed to a kind of rock called sandstone.

Sue's bones changed, too. The layers and layers of sediment pressing down on them caused certain things to happen. Water seeped into the bones, forming new minerals. The bones became heavier, more brittle, and darker brown.

Over millions of years, the Earth changed. Forces inside the Earth moved the land. Mountains formed, with enormous earthquakes and volcanoes in this area. The rivers and seas that covered Sue's homeland dried out. The weather cooled. Sudden rains caused floods, and strong winds blew. The rain and wind cut away the earth, forming the hills and cliffs of modern-day South Dakota. Places that were once deep inside the earth were now near the surface.

Sue's rocky resting place was one of those places. Finally, the rock around her wore away till a few of her bones showed. And along came Susan Hendrickson and Gypsy, hunting for fossils. You know what happened then!

CHAPTER 5

Sue Gets Carried Away

The sandstone hill above Sue had been removed. Now it was time to take her bones out of the ground. Four people from the Black Hills Institute started digging. Using small shovels, picks, and brushes, they carefully dug around the bones. They left the bones in blocks of stone when they could. Later, they would remove that stone with different tools. The block of rock that held Sue's skull and hip bones was taken all in one piece. It weighed four tons!

Bones that looked like they might crack were coated with a special glue. Then each bone or group of bones was covered in foil. The workers applied plaster casts to the bones—

just like a doctor would put on a broken leg. The plaster casts would protect Sue during the trip to the lab.

It took four trucks to hold all of Sue's plaster-covered parts. They were driven back to the Black Hills Institute. The process of cleaning and preparing each bone would begin.

Sue's bones arrived safely. People were hard at work cleaning them when trouble started. Sue was so big and so fantastic that it seemed as if everyone wanted her. The landowner on whose land Sue was found claimed she was his. Because the landowner was part Native American, his tribe, the Sioux, said she was theirs. And the people from the Black Hills Institute who found her thought Sue belonged to them.

The dispute ended up going to court. When it was all over five years later, a judge decided that Sue belonged to the landowner. The landowner decided to sell Sue. She would be sold at an auction.

At an auction, people gather around the object for sale. The auctioneer starts the bidding by calling out a price. People bid higher and higher prices until no one wants to pay any more. The person who offers to pay the most gets to buy the object.

Sue's skull was put on display in a fancy auction house in New York City. People from all over the world came, hoping to buy her.

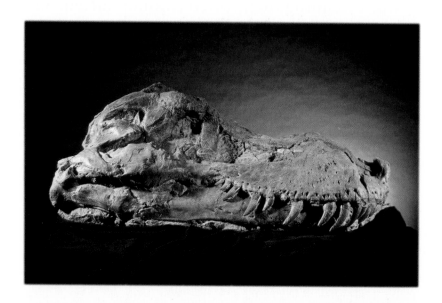

Many places gave money to help the Field Museum buy Sue at the auction, including the McDonald's Corporation, Walt Disney World Resort, the California State University System, and others.

The auction began. People gasped as the bids went up and up and up...over one million dollars, two million dollars, five million dollars. Finally the bidding stopped.

Sold! To whom? The Field Museum in Chicago. For how much? More than eight million dollars!

For the Field Museum, Sue was worth every penny. Now, they would be sure to preserve this very special fossil for scientists to study. And people would be able to visit the museum and see Sue for years to come.

CHAPTER 6

The Work Continues

In 1997, the Field Museum in Chicago became Sue's final home. Scientists there spend every day studying her bones. They think they will still be learning 20 or 100 years from now.

Visitors to the Field Museum can watch as Sue's bones are cleaned. There the McDonald's Fossil Preparation Lab is in full view. The people at work behind the glass are called preparators. Their job is to remove the rock covering Sue's bones so she can be seen and studied.

First they cut away the plaster casts. Next they remove the *matrix*. This is the scientific name for the non-fossil rock that still surrounds the bones. They work very slowly, being extremely careful not to damage anything.

Preparators use a variety of tools to chip off the outer layer of stone. One tool, called an air-scribe, works like a mini-jackhammer. A hard metal tip, pushed by a jet of air, hammers at the stone, chipping it away from the bone.

When only a thin layer of rock is left, prepa-

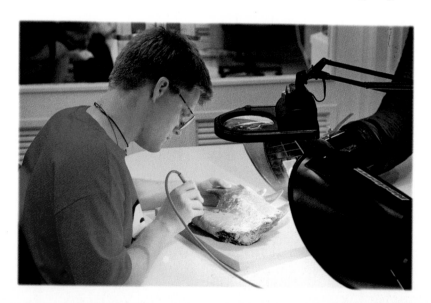

rators use gentler tools. These include tools your dentist uses to clean your teeth — scrapers, probes, and little picks. But mainly, this last layer of matrix is removed by a tiny sandblaster. It uses baking soda instead of sand to wear away the last rock over the bone. Soft paintbrushes sometimes help, too.

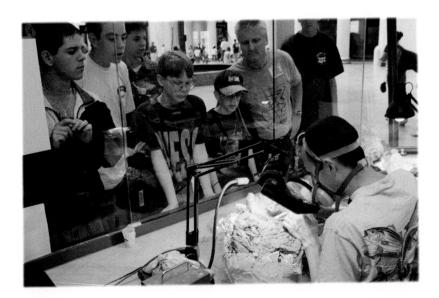

Sue's right arm

Some of Sue's bones are missing. Scientists at the Field Museum will create model bones or make cast copies of bones from other T. rex skeletons to take their place. These bones will be colored reddish brown. This way, visitors will know which bones are real and which ones aren't.

Finally, the bones will be put together. A metal frame will hold up the skeleton. Because Sue's skull is so heavy, it won't be mounted on her skeleton. A lighter cast of the skull will be made for that purpose. Sue's real skull will be placed on the balcony above, overlooking her bones. Eventually, a permanent exhibit hall for all of Sue's bones will be added to the museum.

Field Museum scientists have already learned some important things from studying Sue's bones. Here are just a couple of the things they found out.

• *Sue may have lived longer than any other T. rex ever found.*

Scientists found clues to her age in her bones.

• *Some of her teeth are shaped strangely.*

That's what happens to some teeth of reptiles as they get old. Since Sue was a reptile, scientists think that might be a sign of Sue's old age.

• *Some of Sue's bones grew together.*

The bones of many animals — including people — do that as they age.

• *Most reptiles grow all their lives.*

So the biggest T. rex is probably the oldest. And Sue is the biggest!

From studying Sue's skull, scientists have learned about T. rex brains. The part of Sue's brain that helped her smell was huge. This means Sue had a great sense of smell. It's possible she could smell much better than she could see or hear. T. rex may have used the sense of smell to help track their meals.

What does the Field Museum hope to learn from Sue? Lots! Here are some of the things they are studying.

Did Sue fight with other dinosaurs?

Some of Sue's bones look as though they may have been injured. How might this have happened? Scientists will know more soon.

Just how big was Sue?

Once she's put together, we'll know her exact size. Sue was at least 40 feet long from nose to tip of tail!

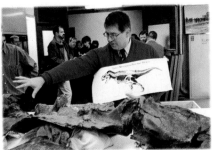

How did T. rex move its heavy body? How fast could it move?

With so many bones from one animal to study, scientists think they can figure this out. They will put information about the size and shape of the bones into a computer. Computer studies will help show how T. rex might have moved.

How is T. rex related to other dinosaurs and to birds?

Scientists will compare Sue's bones to other dinosaurs and their living descendants—birds. Dinosaur species whose bones are a lot like Sue's in certain ways may be closely related to T. rex.

Everyone is very excited about the work at the Field Museum. Susan Hendrickson is paying close attention. She hopes Sue will teach us a great deal. "Sue waited 67 million years to stand up and look at lots of people and have them look at her. People will be awed. The best thing Sue can do is to inspire people to go out and learn more."

That's a big job for a 67 million-year-old fossil. But Sue just might be up to it!